MORDICAI GERSTEIN

Moose, Goose, and Mouse

illustrated by
Mordicai Gerstein
and Jeff Mack

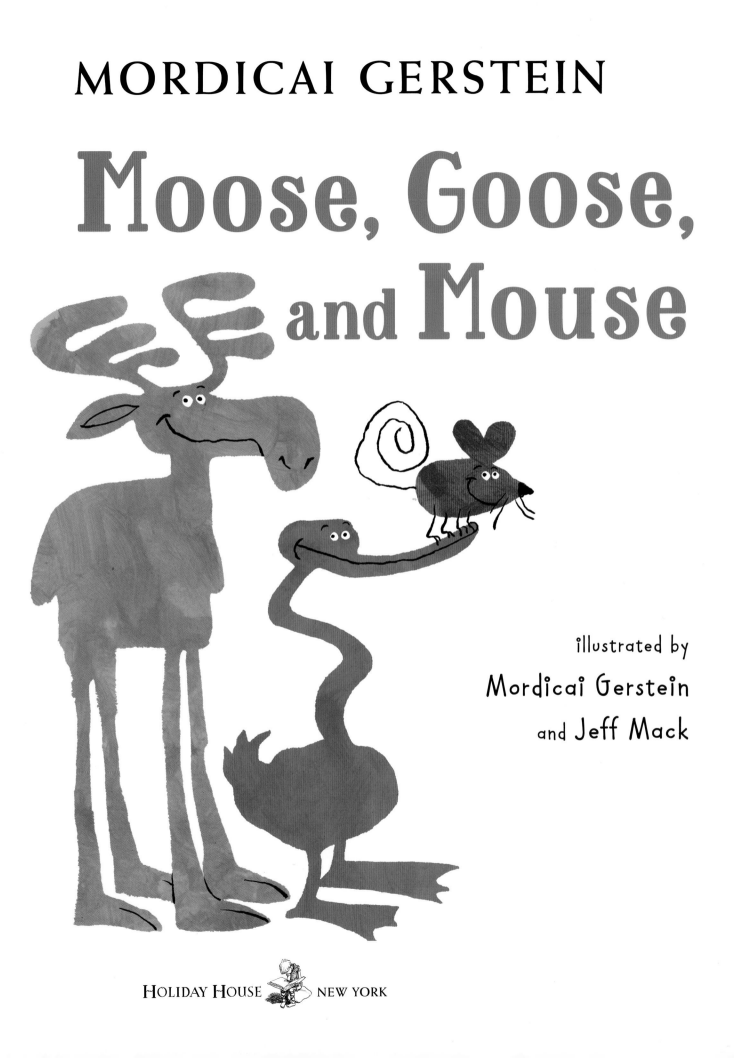

HOLIDAY HOUSE · NEW YORK

Text and art copyright © 2021 by Mordicai Gerstein
Illustrations copyright © 2021 by Mordicai Gerstein and Jeffrey M. Mack
All Rights Reserved
HOLIDAY HOUSE is registered in the U.S. Patent and Trademark Office.
Printed and bound in September 2020 at Leo Paper, Heshan, China.
The artwork was created with ink, pencil, and watercolor on paper and digital collage.
www.holidayhouse.com
First Edition
1 3 5 7 9 10 8 6 4 2

Library of Congress Cataloging-in-Publication Data

Names: Gerstein, Mordicai, author, illustrator. | Mack, Jeff, illustrator.
Title: Moose, Goose, and Mouse / by Mordicai Gerstein ;
illustrated by Mordicai Gerstein and Jeff Mack.
Description: First edition. | New York : Holiday House, [2021] | Audience:
Ages 4–8. | Audience: Grades K–1. | Summary: "Moose, Goose, and Mouse
ride a loose caboose on their way to finding a new house"
—Provided by publisher.
Identifiers: LCCN 2020007657 | ISBN 9780823447602 (hardcover)
Subjects: CYAC: Railroad trains—Fiction. | Moose—Fiction.
Geese—Fiction. | Mice—Fiction. | Dwellings—Fiction. | Humorous stories.
Classification: LCC PZ7.G325 Mm 2021 | DDC [E]—dc23
LC record available at https://lccn.loc.gov/2020007657

ISBN: 978-0-8234-4760-2

For my friend Mordicai —J.M.

Moose, Goose, and Mouse
had a house.

Moose said,
"This house is wet
and old!"

Goose said,
"It's full of mold!"

Mouse said,
"It's very cold!"

Mouse said,
"I want a house that's sunny."

Said Moose,
"I want a house that's funny!"

Goose said,
"I want one with a bunny."

Moose, Goose, and Mouse
took a train in the rain
to look for a house.

They rode in the caboose.

"I like this caboose,"
said Moose and Mouse.

"Me too," said Goose.

Up a hill in the rain
went the train.

But *ooooops*!
The caboose came loose!

The caboose rolled faster down the hill.

Then faster and faster and faster still!

"Yippee!" yelled Moose.
"Wow, what a thrill!"

The caboose rolled up the hill.

The caboose rolled down the hill.

The caboose rolled up the hill.

The caboose rolled down the hill.

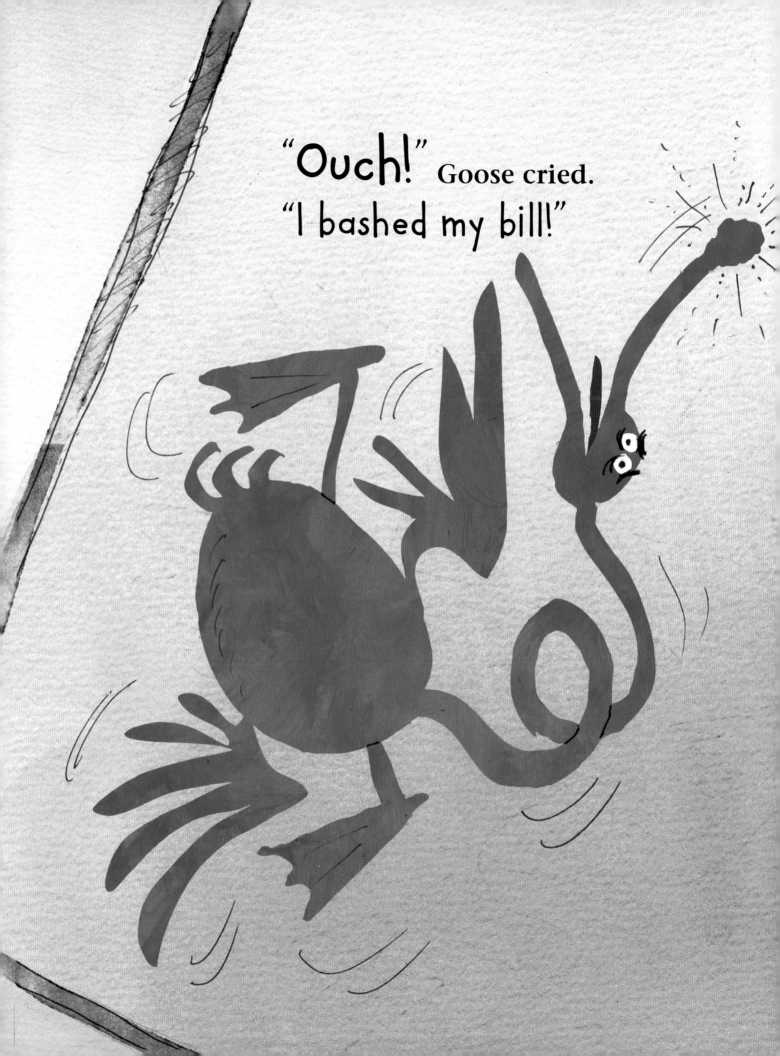

Wailed Mouse
and Moose,
"We're feeling ill!"

Finally,
the train hit a tree near the sea.

Moose said, "It is sunny!"

Goose said,
"This is funny!"

"Is it true?" said Mouse.
"Is that a bunny?"

"It is *true*," said the bunny.

Moose, Goose, and Mouse
have a SUNNY, FUNNY,
loose caboose for a house . . .
with a BUNNY!

A NOTE FROM JEFF MACK

I first met Mordicai Gerstein in January 2010. For nearly ten years, he and I met with four other author friends once a month to talk about our book projects. His creativity was limitless. He loved to explore different ways to make pictures. He wrote in just about every genre of children's literature.

Eventually, Mordicai and I started having lunch together. During one of our lunches, he said he had written a story about a moose, a goose, and a mouse who take a wild train ride in the rain and end up living inside the caboose. He was experimenting with a new art style and he asked me to help him figure out the technique.

A few days later, I went to Mordicai's home studio. We scanned scraps of painted paper and tried out different collage techniques on his computer until we found exactly the look he had in mind. Over the next few weeks, we talked on the phone about the variations that he could achieve with the new technique.

Then, one day, he emailed me to ask how I would feel about finishing the book for him. I knew he had been fighting cancer. Now he was having fewer good days than bad. It was getting too hard to work. I felt honored that he trusted me to complete the work on this last book. Of course, I said yes.

I took his drawings and sketches, and began scanning them into my computer along with some scraps of paper that I painted. Then I assembled the illustrations in my own studio the way we had in his. Over the next couple of weeks, I brought my laptop to Mordicai's bedside, and we worked together, adjusting colors and details, until the images looked just right. We finished about half of the illustrations that way, and then Mordicai said, "Okay, you're on your own now."